CHRIS GETS THE
HiCCUPS!

Hic!

AL ARGO
ILLUSTRATED BY ANDRESSA MEISSNER

BUY GIVE 1

Published by Positive Impact Kids

PO Box 555, Ohatchee, Al 36271 USA

Copyright © Al Argo 2018

At Positive Impact Kids, when you purchase our children's books in any format, print, e-book or audiobook, we match it and give a new or used book to a school, library, child or family in a developing nation.

Our goal is to give 1 million books away in the next 10 years. Your reviews on Amazon, Goodreads, Audible and recommendations on social media can help us reach more people and ultimately give more books away overseas! THANK YOU!

If you'd like to donate gently used kids books (or tax-deductible cash to help with shipping overseas) you may do so!
Positive Impact Kids Book Club - C/O Every Nation Education,
PO Box 116 - Falcon, NC 28342 USA

Cover Design and Illustrations by Andressa Meissner

ISBN 978-1981314270

10 9 8 7 6 5 4 3 2 1

First published by Positive Impact Kids 2018
Printed in the USA

DEDICATED TO CHRIS, NATALEE, EMILY, KALEB
AND ALL MY GREAT FRIENDS IN AUSTRALIA.

ALSO DEDICATED TO ALEX, CHANDLER,
FUTURE-GRANDCHILDREN AND ALL MY NIECES,
NEPHEWS, COUSINS, SECOND-COUSINS AND
FRIENDS THE WORLD OVER!

THANKS ALSO TO CHRIS, JANNA, ROBIN AND
HALEY FOR HELPING EDIT. YOU ARE ALL
APPRECIATED!

I ONCE HAD A FRIEND WHO HAD
TIME ON HIS HAND,

TO TRAVEL FAR
AND WIDE
TO ANOTHER LAND.

WHEN I
MET HIM,
HE ALSO
MET ME

AND TOGETHER
THE WORLD
WE WANTED
TO SEE.

HE SAW MY HOME,
WE SAW THE
WORLD

AND ONE DAY
I TRAVELED TO HIS
DOWN UNDER
LAND.

THE KANGAROOS
WERE SWIFT,

THE KOALA BEARS
WERE MEAN,

BUT THE ICE CREAM
WAS THE BEST I'D
EVER EATEN OR SEEN.

LEMON-LIME
AND BITTERS WAS
THE FLAVOR JUST
FOR ME.

NOW, I
WILL FOREVER CRAVE
THAT ONE, YOU SEE.

BUT AS WE
FINISHED
ANOTHER SCOOP
OF FREEZING
ICE-CREAM,

HICCUP
HIC
HICCUP
HICCUP
HIC
HICCUP
HIC
HICCUP
HIC
Hic!
HICCUP
HIC

HIC
CUP
!!!

HIC
HIC
HIC
HIC
HICCUP
HICCUP
HIC
HIC
HICCUP
HICCUP
HIC
HIC
HIC
HIC

I THOUGHT HE'D WANT THEM TO
VERY QUICKLY END,

SO ALL OF A SUDDEN,
WITH NO
THOUGHT
OR A CARE,

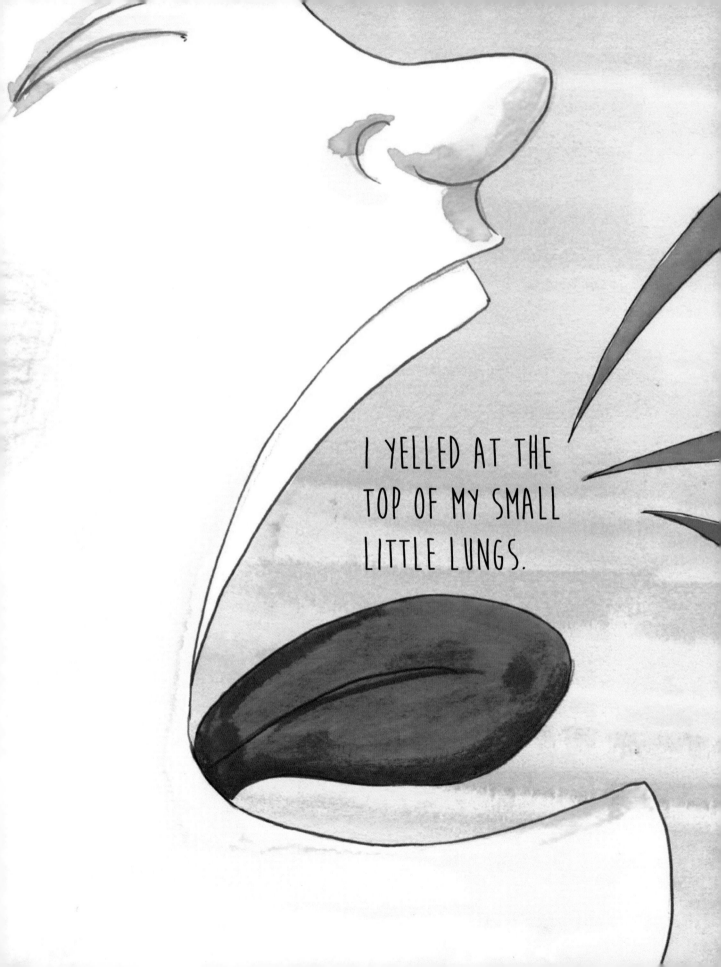

I YELLED AT THE
TOP OF MY SMALL
LITTLE LUNGS.

I LET A YELP
COME OFF THE
TIP OF MY TONGUE.

BOOOOO!!

THE LOOK ON HIS FACE WAS OF UTTER DELIGHT.

YOU SEE, HIS HICCUPS WERE QUICKLY GONE, WHEN I GAVE HIM A FRIGHT!

THIS IS THE
TRUE STORY
OF MY DOWN UNDER
FRIEND,

HIS NAME IS REALLY CHRIS, AND YOU'VE REACHED THE END!

HUMOROUS HICCUP FACTS!

1) SOME PEOPLE SAY HICCUPS ARE A SIGN **YOU ARE GROWING!**

2) THAT MAY NOT BE TRUE, BUT IT IS TRUE TODDLERS HICCUP MORE THAN ADULTS AND YOU COULD HAVE HAD THE HICCUPS **BEFORE YOU WERE EVER BORN!**

3) THERE ONCE WAS A MAN, CHARLES OSBORNE, **WHO HICCUPED FOR 69 YEARS!**

4) DON'T WORRY! THE AVERAGE CASE OF HICCUPS ONLY **LAST 5 MINUTES!**

5) **BE CAREFUL!** SCARING SOMEONE WITH THE HICCUPS COULD CAUSE **SKID MARKS!**

97980724R00020

Made in the USA
Columbia, SC
19 June 2018